MW00875983

The Secret Lives of Mothers

By B.M. Green

This book is a work of fiction. Any names, characters, companies, organizations, places, events, locales, and incidents are either used in a fictitious manner or are fictional. Any resemblance to actual persons, living or dead, actual companies or organizations, or actual events is purely coincidental.

Copyright © 2023 by Brittany Green. All rights reserved. No part of this work may be reproduced, stored in a retrieval system or transmitted in any form by any means, electronic, mechanical, photocopying, recording, or otherwise, without written permission of the publisher.

Cover Design by Brittany Green in collaboration with WOMBO Dream.

This book is not endorsed by or affiliated with the musical artist mentioned. All rights to music reserved by the artist and there label label.

Table of contents:

slay hy

Trigger Warning:

This book covers sensitive topics such as teenage pregnancy, sexual assault, pregnancy and loss, and suicide. These are real issues that mothers face. Some of the stories may be triggering. Please remember to be gentle with yourselves, show yourself grace, practice self-care and please reach out to someone for help if you or someone you know is experiencing one of these issues.

If you are in America please utilize the below resources:

American Pregnancy Association toll-free teen pregnancy hotline 1-800-672-2296

National Sexual Assault Hotline: 1-800-656-HOPE

988 Suicide and Crisis Lifeline: 988

Alexa, play A Mothers Prayer by K. Michelle

1.

The Parent Vow

F or this child I prayed, and the Lord hath given me my petition which I asked of Him. -1 Samuel 1:27

Gazing into the crib, she could not believe that he was finally here. His soft whimpers as he sleeps, sounding like the most beautiful symphony filling her ears. He was a physical manifestation of every prayer she had prayed to God for a child. Gently touching his head to not wake him but to feel him near she whispered....

Hello, I've been waiting for you.
I've had dreams about the day you'd make your debut!
I've counted your toes and fingers in my mind.
My beautiful baby, perfectly designed!
Your presence is more than I could dream or wish.
You are the most precious gift.
Your smile brightens my darkest day.
Your cry makes me want to make sure no harm comes your way.
For you, I've prayed and God answered me.
You have set my unconditional love free.
So I make these vows to you,
From parent to child they will remain true.
Nothing will ever take my love away.
My love is yours until my very last day.

I will kiss every boo-boo and help you up after every fall.

I will wipe your tears and answer every call.

I will teach you about kindness, strength, and compassion.

I will nurture your gifts and encourage you to follow your passions.

I will raise you up with loving discipline.

And when you need to talk, know that I am always listening.

I'll be honest with you because I know I may not always get it right.

But trust every day I'm trying with all my might,

To be what it is you need me to be

And I'll never give up, that is a guarantee.

I have been waiting for you.

You have made my dreams come true with your debut.

I still can't believe God entrusted you to me.

But with God, I know I could never disagree.

So I stand tall and deeply rooted like a tree,

And to you I make this decree,

I'll love you more and more each day

This is a vow that will never fade away.

Hey Google, play What's Going On
by Remy Ma ft Keyshia Cole

2.

Teen Mom

"Ew, what are you eating?" I asked my sister Tara covering my nose in disgust as she entered our room carrying a takeout bag.

"What do you mean? This is what we always get from *Albertos*. I got you that burrito you like." She replied looking at me quizzically.

"You did?" I said putting my hand out and motioning for her to give me the takeout bag.

"It doesn't smell funny to you?" I asked as I took the wrapping off the burrito, smelling it before I took a bite. " I barely got one chew in when I said "omg I'm about to throw up" and ran to the bathroom to do just that. On my knees in front of the toilet puking my brains out I could feel my sister's eyes on me. "Girl, I told you something was wrong with that food!" I said to Tara.

"Umm hmm, nothing is wrong with the food Amina but there might be something wrong with you." She replied, eyeing me suspiciously.

"What do you mean? Nothing is wrong with me" I said, getting up from the ground and immediately going to brush my teeth.

"For the past few days you have been uber-sensitive to smell, throwing up, and getting sick. At first, I thought you just had a bug so I was trying to social distance, but now I'm pretty sure what you have isn't contagious. Amina, I think you're pregnant!" She said with a look of concern on her face.

As I finished brushing my teeth, I glanced at my reflection in the mirror thinking Tara's statement was completely absurd. There was no way I could be pregnant. Our mother, Diane Daniels, had Tara and my future picked out before we could even walk. We would both go to her alma mater, Clark Atlanta University, an HBCU, or a Historically Black College/University. I would attend first, being a year older than Tara, and would pledge Alpha Kappa Alpha Sorority, Inc and formulate strong relationships with all the girls in the sorority so when Tara arrived a year later they would happily welcome her in too. Tara was going to pursue a degree in aerospace engineering and I was going to work on becoming the next Oliva Pope with my criminal justice major. I couldn't wait to walk the same halls my mother did during her undergrad and continue the Daniel women's legacy of being an AKA. This dream may have started as my mother's but I certainly adopted it as my own. Any moment now my acceptance letter would be arriving and I would be one step closer to making our dream a reality. Babies did not fit into that plan until well after I passed the bar, give or take a year or two so my future husband and I have some "us" time as a newlywed couple before expanding our family!

"What!? There is like literally no way I'm pregnant. Why would you even say something like that?" I asked her, brushing past her and heading to the kitchen to get some water.

Following behind me she said "So you think I don't know that you and Cameron hooked up after homecoming? Talking about you were sleeping over at Amy's when Amy was with me and the rest of the crew at IHOP and you and Cameron were nowhere to be found. It didn't take a rocket scientist Amina and that's coming from someone who wants to be a rocket scientist one day" I rolled my eyes at her.

Cameron had gotten his older brother to get us a room at the hotel our homecoming dance was held at. He made it so romantic just like in the movies with flowers and candles everywhere it was easy to get caught up in the moment.

"So what, we made love. That doesn't mean I'm pregnant" I replied.

"Made love?" Tara literally laughed her ass off "You're 17, you and Cameron were not making love. You were straight fu.."

"Ok ok, we had sex is that better?"

Tara continued laughing "Yeah well whatever you two did got you pregnant"

Looking down at my flat stomach I wondered if what my sister said could be true. Was I pregnant? I had been super sensitive to smell lately and out of nowhere I was always nauseous. *But I'm only 17. I have so much to do before I become a mother.* Teen pregnancy was not a part of our mother's dream for my life and it certainly was not a part of my plan for me either. I could feel my heartbeat increase as panic began to set in. *There is no way I could be pregnant!*

"Ah shit," Tara said " I can see you over there overthinking. Sit down" She told me as I went to take a seat at our dining room table. "Don't panic, I mean I'm pretty sure you're pregnant but just so we know for certain I'll get you a pregnancy test. If the test is positive, you have options. If you decide to keep it, I'll be with you when you tell mom and Cameron and if you decide not to, I still have that planned parenthood info sheet we got in Sex ED, we could call them." Tell Cameron and mom, call Planned Parenthood I thought.

"Nope this isn't happening. I'm not pregnant." I said walking out of the kitchen back to my room and slamming the door. This was much too much to process for one afternoon. Sure I haven't been feeling well but I have also been super busy. I mean it's my senior year and these AP classes have been kicking my butt. Maybe I just needed some rest. Yeah, I thought to myself, I just need a nap and I will wake up refreshed and this nightmare will be over.

A few hours later

"Hey sleepyhead," my sister said, pushing me to wake up.

"What," I said groggily from my nap.

"I got you something," She said, pulling out a pregnancy test.

Rolling over I said "I'm not taking that because I know I'm not pregnant. Now go away I still smell that burrito from early on your breath and it's making me" I paused catching myself before I said the words sick or nauseous. "You just stink."

"Yeah whatever. Humor me. Just take the test and prove me wrong." When I didn't budge she said, "Take the test and I'll call Luther Maxwell and ask him out on a date" I turned around so quickly we both almost fell out of the bed.

"Fine," I said, snatching the test from her hands. "Only because I want to see you ask Luther out!" I smirked and headed to the bathroom to take the test. *There is no way I am pregnant and seeing Tara ask Luther out would be worth it, she has been crushing on him since 6th grade!* I took the stick-like test out of the box along with the instructions, doing a quick glance over them, I sat down to pee on the stick.

"You know this was a total waste of time right?" I said handing her the test.

"Eww, did you wipe this thing down with a Clorox wipe before you gave it to me? I love you and all but I'm not trying to hold your pee, Amina." She said just as our mother walked into the house.

"Hey girls," She said, walking past us into the kitchen.

"Hide it," I whispered.

"Amina come here I have something for you" our mother yelled and Tara and I both nervously walked into the kitchen. "Look what came in the mail today!" She said excitedly, handing me a big envelope from Clark Atlanta University. "You know what they say, if the envelope is big that's a good sign"

I smiled wide and eagerly opened the envelope reading in silence until I reached the part I was looking for "I got in! I got in!" My Mom ran to hug me as Tara looked down then headed towards the stairs leaving Mom and me alone in the kitchen.

"I knew you would. Baby girl, I am so proud of you! Another panther in the house" Mom said, celebrating. "Oh, we are going out tonight. We have to commemorate this moment. Let me call your dad, oh and my mom she's going to flip!" Mom said reaching for her phone and leaving the kitchen to make her calls.

Excitedly I ran upstairs to find Tara. "Hey, why'd you leave? Can you believe I got in?" I asked.

"Of course I can believe you got in Amina, you're almost as smart as me," She said with a weak smile.

"Almost? Girl I am where you get your smarts from" still smiling extra hard from my acceptance letter. "Mom is taking us out to dinner to celebrate."

"And there are so many things to celebrate," Tara said " I mean you get into your top school and you're going to be a mom!" The smile immediately left my face.

"Stop playing Tara, don't ruin this moment for me," I said.

"I'm not playing" Tara pulled out the pregnancy test and handed it to me "You're pregnant sis," She said matter-of-factly.

"It's wrong," I said, throwing the test to the ground. "It's a false positive," I said walking over to my bed.

"Girl, it's 99% accurate," Tara said, rubbing my back as I buried my face into my pillow as the tears that began to cloud my eyes.

"This can't be happening," I said.

"Girls, get ready! I think tonight calls for Ruth Chris!" Mom yelled from downstairs.

"I can't go," I said to Tara, trying and failing to hold back my tears.

"Of course, you can" She replied "Steak doesn't make you sick, Mexican food does," She said laughing. When I didn't laugh with her she continued to rub my back and said "Look, I got your back. I'll be with you when you're ready to tell Mom" I cried louder thinking of what our mom would do to me when she found out. This was not a part of our plan "If you decide not to keep it, I'll go with you and hold your hand. If you do keep it, I might babysit sometimes. Whatever you need, I got you." she said, pulling me into an embrace that told me no matter what my sister would be there for me.

"Let go girls!" Mom happily screamed at us.

"Look at the bright side," Tara said while walking towards the bedroom door.

"What's that?" I asked, still trying to contain all my emotions.

"Now you get to see me ask Luther out. I seriously can't believe I said I'd do that. But don't worry, I promise not to get pregnant." Turning to look at me she said "Too soon?" and I threw my pillow at her, laughing, "My bad, it's def too soon. Come on, let's celebrate your college acceptance. We can figure out that other thing later." Tara said, gesturing towards my stomach before walking out of the room screaming "Coming Mom!"

Six Years Later

"Amina Daniels" echoed through the convention hall as I made my way across the stage shaking the dean of the Syracuse College of Law's hand. I entered the 3 + 3 acceleration admissions program between Clark Atlanta University and Syracuse University College of Law and was able to complete my undergrad, Juris, and master's degree in just six years. Looking to my left I saw my family cheering loudly as I accepted my diploma. My mother, grandmother, and sister looked at me with admiration and my heart swelled knowing I did not only myself proud but my family as well. I had followed the plan and now I was a lawyer.

Mom wrapped me in a warm embrace as soon as she spotted me in the sea of college graduates.

"I am so proud of you. My baby, the lawyer!" She said enthusiastically. "You hear that" She yelled to no one in particular " My daughter is a lawyer honey!" She said looking at my grandmother and family members.

As they continued to celebrate I heard a little girl cry out "Mommy" Turning to the sound I looked into the eyes of a beautiful five-year-old who rushed past me to hug another graduate.

"Mommy, I saw you on the big screen and they said your name really loud," the little girl told her mom. "Did you hear me scream for you?" She asked looking up at her mother expectantly. I watched the exchange between mother and daughter and it was as if everyone else disappeared and I could only see them. I could only see myself. I could only see my child that wasn't there. I never told my mother about my pregnancy but I did tell Cameron. He was supportive at first and accompanied Tara and me to the abortion clinic when I terminated the pregnancy.

A few days later, he told me that he got accepted to LSU and that he thought it was best for us to just cut our losses and move on. I agreed, I had a plan to stick to and I did just that. That was how I honored our baby, by following the plan and doing what I said I'd do. I was brought back to reality with the touch of Tara's hand on my shoulder.

"You okay sis," Tara asked me while also staring at the mother-daughter scene before us.

"Yeah, I'm fine," I said, turning my back on the little girl to face my family. "Everything happened just the way we planned."

Hey Siri, play Sometimes I Feel like a Motherless Child by Jazmin Sullivan

3.

Neglectful Mom

"Mom, can I talk to you for a sec?" Jamie said to her mother. "I'm on the phone" she whispered before continuing her conversation. "Yes, Mr. Oshiro, my firm is committed to ensuring this merger is successful. You have nothing to worry about."

Jamie stared at her mother thinking that maybe if she were a client her mother would pay attention to her. She never felt as important to her mother as her job clearly was. But this was an emergency. She needed her mother to listen. She needed her mother to be her mother and just for a moment pretend that she cared about her too.

"Mom, I really need to talk to you," Jamie said pleading with her mother to hang up the phone. It was almost 9 pm and while most households would be winding down around that time, Jamie's mother would usually spend that time picking up the work she should have left at the office. She'd return home from work every day around 7 pm or 8 pm with some takeout, say hi to Jamie and kiss her little brother James then head to her office. Most days when Jamie woke up at 6 am to get ready for school, her mother was already gone.

Her mother was determined to have it all without a man. A single mother by choice, she felt that Jamie and James completed her image as an uncompromising businesswoman with her own family. While Jamie understood that as a partner at her law firm, *Daniels, Jacolby & West*, and Head of Merger & Acquisitions, her mother had a very demanding job, she wished her mother compromised less of her time with her children and a tad bit more of her time at work. Her hours could be long and unpredictable and Jamie got used to playing mom to her brother James in their mother's absence. Jamie made sure he was up for school in the morning, that he brushed his teeth, ate breakfast, and was ready for the car his mother arranged to take them to school. Jamie helped him with homework, tucked him in at night, and checked the closest to ensure him that there were no monsters inside. But after Jamie would ensure James was out for the night she would go to her room and cry. Jamie was an independent thirteen-year-old, she had to be since her mother relied on her heavily to take care of her little brother, but Jamie was keeping a secret from her mother that was proving to be too much for her to carry on her own. She needed her mom to listen.

"Mom, please" Jamie begged as tears welled up in her eyes. Her mother put one finger up signaling to Jamie to give her a second. Jamie could no longer contain herself as frustrated tears began to escape from her eyes. Her mother looked up at her with a confused look but continued her conversation with her client. Why couldn't I have a regular mom? Jamie thought as she walked away from her mother towards her room. Jamie entered her room and went straight for her desk frantically searching as the tears blurred her vision. When she found what she was looking for she caught a glimpse of herself in the mirror on her desk. "No tears, no fears, just preserve" she repeated the mantra her grandmother had taught her when she was younger.

"Make her hear you, Jamie!" She whispered to herself as she did her best to clean her face. Holding the foreign object was still surreal to Jamie but she hoped it would finally get her mother's attention. Walking back into her mother's office, Jamie could hear her say

"Thank you again, Mr. Oshiro. I will call you tomorrow with the update" Without hesitation Jamie slammed the object on her mother's desk hoping it would prevent her mom from hopping on yet another work call.

"What is wrong with you Jamie? I told you about interrupting me when I am on calls. And what is this?" Her mother paused, picking up the pregnancy test and looking at Jamie. "What is this Jamie? Are you…are you pregnant? I didn't even know you were having sex!"

"I'm not!" Jamie yelled.

"Well, then what the hell is this?" her mom yelled "Huh, immaculate conception? Where did you even get a pregnancy test?" She asked angrily.

"I used the money you left me to pick up dinner at the diner down the street and got the test from the store instead," Jamie replied somberly.

"I can't believe you would be this stupid Jamie. After everything I have done to give you and your brother the best life has to offer and you squander it away like this? You haven't heard of a condom?" Jamie's mother was screaming.

"This isn't my fault, it's yours Mom!" Jamie yelled back.

"Mine? Please Jamie enlighten me. How the hell is this my fault?" Jamie paused and repeated her grandmother's mantra to herself "No tears, no fears, just preserve"

"Two months ago you brought your clients over for dinner. You said they came into town last minute and wanted to discuss business but they didn't want to go to a fancy restaurant so you invited them to our house. You stuck me with their son, remember? You told me to take him downstairs to the den while you all worked on whatever you were working on. Well, when we got downstairs I asked him if he wanted to watch a movie. He told me to put on whatever but he was more interested in me. I asked him why and he said that you told him that I would take really good care of him, you know keep him entertained while you guys worked. Then he scooched next to me on the couch. I tried to back away but he just got closer. I told him you meant I'd keep him company like watching tv and hanging out until you guys were done but he said he didn't want to watch tv. Next thing I know he was kissing me. I had never been kissed before so I went with it until his hands started touching me and I started to feel uncomfortable. I tried to push him away but he was stronger than me and he pushed me on the floor and put his hands up my dress." Unable to control her emotions any longer Jamie turned her back to her mother and the tears began to fall.

"I said please don't. I'm a virgin, I haven't been touched there. He just smiled and said don't worry I will be gentle. Then he just did it. I wanted to yell but I knew you wouldn't hear me since you got the basement soundproofed after James kept interrupting your work last year by playing too loud. When they left I tried to tell you but you were too busy on work calls or drafting some contract or something that was clearly more important than me. Every day for a week after I tried to wait for an opportunity to tell you but you were always too busy. So I tried to forget about it. But then I noticed my period didn't come and I started feeling really sick" Turning to her mother Jamie's voice cracked as she said, "Mommy, what do I do?" Jamie and her mother stood face to face, both of their faces swollen with sorrow.

"Jamie" her mother whispered, taking a step closer to her, but before she could say anything else her work phone rang.

She better not answer it!.

Hey Alexa, play Baby Mama
by Three Six Mafia & La Chat

1.

Toxic BM

"Yeah, girl I'm on my way to that nigga house right now. I need a break, shit" Yandy yelled into the phone. "Yep girl, 'cause it ain't just on me. These niggas think they can do whatever they want. Not messing me though, I don't know who he thinks he is messing with because I ain't the one or the two" Yandy laughed. "ISAIAH!" "Hold on girl" "Boy have you lost your mind? Sit down" "Yeah girl, this little boy in the back seat trying to take off his seatbelt. Hardheaded just like his daddy. So anyway, we hitting *Supreme* tonight? I'm trying to fuck up the night like Beyonce" Yandy said doing a little twerk in her seat. "Oh hell no" Yandy said, pulling up to her baby daddy's house. "Girl, I am about to go OFF. I'm pulling up to this niggas house and he got the nerve to have that bitch car in the driveway. She bet not be here because it's on sight if she is. Let me call you back!"

Bryon - Then

Yandy and Bryon met six years ago while she was working at The Pretty Kitty, their local strip club. Bryon was immediately mesmerized by Yandy's stage presence, her curves, and her ability to move her body to a beat like she was made of the melody. He would go to the club every Thursday and watch her dance. He had recently moved back home after losing his job and being at The Pretty Kitty watching Yandy was the only place he felt good. Yandy had become his therapy and he never missed a session.

"Your usual again?" the waitress said to him one night.

"Uh, yeah just a beer" he replied keeping his eyes on Yandy. The waitress grabbed a beer that was already on her tray anticipating his answer.

"Look, I know you come here to see Yandy, I get it she's beautiful and all but you seem like a good one so I'm just going to tell you" Bryon pulled his attention away from Yandy who was with another man a couple of tables away, he was very interested in what the waitress had to tell him about the woman he had been fantasizing about the past couple of weeks.

"Yandy is a lifer, she'll never leave the pole. She doesn't know anything other than this life. Even if you got her to fall for you, she wouldn't be able to help swallowing you up and spitting you out. You're not ready for a girl like her. There are other girls in here that might be up your alley but Yandy ain't one of them."

"Like you?" he asked with a slight edge to his tone. Clearly, the waitress was hating on Yandy. Maybe while Bryon was busy looking at Yandy the waitress was busy looking at him, he thought. "Look, my bad, I appreciate the warning, but I got it," He told her.

"Okay, don't say I didn't warn you," The waitress said walking away.

Now

Yandy pulled up to the house parking in front of the driveway instead of on the street which had plenty of open spots. Taking off her seatbelt she opened her car door and began walking to the front of the house. Turning around to see Isaiah was not following her she yelled,

"Isaiah, you see me walking to the door, get out of the car boy!" Isaiah, four years old, knew exactly how to unbuckle his seatbelt and excitedly did so and happily ran up to his mom. Yandy banged on the door "Bryon, open this door" A few seconds later Bryon emerged. He was still as beautiful as the first day Yandy met him at The Pretty Kitty. He was wearing sweatpants and no shirt and Yandy could tell he had been working out because his mahogany-colored skin glistened with perspiration. Damn, he was fine, she thought to herself.

"Dang girl, why are you banging on my door like you're the police or something?"

"Daddy!" Isaiah said happy to see his dad. Bryon looked down at him and smiled "What up Lil man." Refocusing her attention Yandy said,

"Fuck all that, is that bitch here?" Bryon exhaled loudly, grabbing his head out of frustration.

"You know she is here, Yandy. She lives here. You know we have been living together for the past year."

"A year, Bryon? You've been living with this trick for a year?"

"Yandy why are you like this, man? Why can't you just drop off my son and be on your way? I'm not even trying to fight with you."

"So you must got extra money now, you know since you live with that bitch. You split rent and shit, right? You should be able to break me off something."

"Girl, you get a check every month!"

"Clearly it ain't enough. Your son is expensive and if she is going to be around him playing step mom then she should be paying me too!"

Then

After attending for a few nights, he finally gained the courage to speak to her. "How much for a lap dance?" Bryon asked Yandy. Yandy looked him up and down, she had noticed him and more importantly, she had noticed him noticing her. Bryon wasn't like the other men that visited the club, he wasn't overly aggressive with the dancers, he wasn't getting sloppy drunk and handsy, and he didn't have that caveman "I am man, give me pussy" attitude. Bryon was different. Sweet even.

"Why don't we go to a private room, huh? It's much quieter there," she replied, grabbing his hand and leading him down a hallway. Once in the VIP room Yandy turned on some slow jams and started to move her body seductively. To her surprise, Bryon raised his hand to stop her.

"I have seen you dance and we both know you are amazing at what you do but I was wondering if you'd…" He paused before saying.

"If you'd let me get to know you. The real you." Yandy had been in the business long enough to know that some men could fall in love with the fantasy. Bryon wasn't the first man to approach her talking about "Let me get to know you ma" and each time Yandy collected their money and moved on to the next. But this time caused her to pause. There was a sincerity in Bryon's eyes she hadn't witnessed before. Something that told her he was different. He could be the one to change things for her. If she let him.

Yandy - Then

Yandy and Bryon were inseparable after that night in the VIP room. For the first time in Yandy's life, she had a man that was fully hers. Bryon was not a messy situationship or a sneaky link, he was her man. *HER MAN.* She could not believe that she had gotten into a relationship with a man she met at the club. And when the girls told her if it was real it would only be a matter of time before he made her choose between him and the pole she would brush them off knowing her man was different. He loved her just as she was and that included her being a dancer. Bryon was just different in the best ways. That's why a year into their relationship Yandy wasn't even mad when she noticed she had missed her period. Bryon was the one for her and she couldn't wait to have his child.

Yandy and Bryon lay in bed. "You think you'd ever stop stripping?" Bryon asked her. Turning to look at him Yandy replied

"You want me to stop? I thought you were okay with it?"

"I was okay with it but I am in a better place now. Financially, I can take care of us. You could go back to school if you wanted. You said you used to want to be a nurse, you could do that. I would support you. We could have a real family. Do you want that? A family with me and our baby, I mean?" Bryon asked her, rubbing her stomach.

Yandy had already planned to take a break from stripping after her first trimester. She thought nothing was more ghetto than a baby-bumping stripper shaking ass in the club, but she loved dancing and didn't want to give it up just because Bryon got some fancy IT job. What did she look like going back to school anyway? No one in her family went to college. They were all hustlers and taught her to be one too. Hustling is all she had ever known. She was a pro at using her body to get what she wanted. Hell her body got her Bryon. She was still in her prime and just because she was having his baby didn't mean he was going to change her. He was going to have to accept her for the woman she was now, not for the woman he thought she could be later because Yandy didn't believe that woman could ever exist outside of his dreams.

Bryon's POV

I wanted to love Yandy but she wouldn't let me. It was like the more successful I got the more she pulled away insisting she didn't need me and she could take care of herself. I wasn't trying to save her from her old life, I was just trying to build a new life together. But the harder I tried the more I came to realize that Camille, that waitress, was right. Yandy did swallow me up and spit me right back out and now she is determined to make my life a living hell just because Camille and I got together. Talking about I gave Camille her life, nah she gave Camille her life. She told me that I needed a girl that wanted a husband and a family. A woman that wanted to work a regular job and be taken care of by her man. She said that wasn't the life for her. So why is she so mad that after she broke up with me, I went and got a lady she told me to get!? Man, this shit is crazy. I am trapped with this girl for the rest of my life. Trying to play nice so I can be a part of Isaiah's life while Yandy is determined to make it hard for me every step of the way just because I know deep down she wishes she stayed with me. That she took the path Camille did when she left The Pretty Kitty and went back to school and became a teacher. But she made her choice and I made mine and now I just wish she would move on so we could raise our son in peace.

Yandy's POV

Bryon thinks I regret leaving him. Like I'd ever want that cookie cutter stepford wife's life he has with that wack ass bitch Camille. My life is way better than that. I got niggas tryna wife me everyday at The Pretty Kitty. I can have my choice of men. If I wanted that life I could have had it.

I could have had it.

They both know that little perfect world they have other there, he built that shit for me! That was my house. That was my car. He was *MY MAN*. That was my life! Now she has it but it's whatever. I always knew that hoe wanted to be me. She can have my sloppy seconds. But Isaiah is mine and she'll never be his mom and she will never replace me in Bryon's life. They could break up tomorrow but me, Isaiah and Bryon will be family forever. I have no intentions of making life easy for Bryon and Camille.

But if somewhere in the future the stars align and Bryon wants his *real* family back....

I would easily return to him.

Now

Bryon rolled his eyes "Look man, can I just get my son? I told my mom I was going to bring him by since she hasn't seen him in a while."

"I get to see grandma!" Isaiah yelled excitedly.

Yandy placed her hand on Isaiah and pushed him behind her. "I don't know, does he get to see grandma?" She placed her hand out towards Bryon waiting for him to pay for her to leave. To Yandy nothing in life was free, not even the time her son spent with his father.

"Yo, you're really trying to charge me to spend time with my son?" Bryon asked. When Yandy did not flinch, Bryon rolled his eyes and pulled out his wallet. Through clenched teeth he muttered, "I only got $100 on me."

Yandy snatched the money from his hand "That's fine, I'll get the rest when you drop him off. Turning to Isaiah, Yandy kneeled in front of her son "Look don't go in that house telling them none of my business and you bet not call that hoe in there Mom!"

"I won't Mommy," Isaiah said, kissing her on the cheek. "Love you, bye-bye," he said, running into his dad's arms. Bryon quickly picked up his son and slammed the door, wondering how he ever procreated with a woman like Yandy.

Bixby, play Heaven by Beyonce

5.

Empty Mom

"Ow," I screeched out in pain.

"Michelle, baby you okay?" Nolan, my husband asked, turning his position in our bed to look at me.

"I think so," I replied. "I just felt a sharp pain in my side" I had fibroids and usually felt this kind of sharp pain right before I started my period but I hadn't experienced it in the three months since I found out I was pregnant. "I'll be ok, baby. I think it's my fibroids acting up again. Sorry to wake you up." I said.

"Let me make you some tea and get you some medicine for the pain. It's time to get ready for work anyway," he said.

I smiled up at him saying thank you as another wave of pain hit me. It was six AM and I had to get ready for work as well. Praying a hot shower and some Tylenol will do the trick, I got out of bed and decided to soldier through my pain. This was the longest work day of my entire life. I would be fine for a few minutes then out of nowhere it was like my uterus was hit by an eighteen-wheeler. Was this my fibroids or something else? The Tylenol was useless as inconsistent bouts of pain sent shock waves throughout my body for the duration of the day. I am still not sure how I completed my work day.

"Honey, I have been feeling miserable all day. I think I am going to go to the hospital just to make sure everything is ok with the baby. Hopefully, they can help me with this pain."

"Do you want me to come pick you up from work and drive you over?" Nolan asked Michelle.

"No, it's ok. I'm in the car heading over now. Meet me there?"

"I'm on my way," he said and we hung up the phone. Arriving at the hospital my husband ran to my car to help me into the doctor's office.

"How may I help you?" a security officer stopped us before we could enter the building.

"My wife. There's something wrong with her. She's pregnant and in pain and needs to see a doctor," was my Nolan's reply.

"Ma'am, I can get you a wheelchair and help you in, unfortunately, due to covid sir you can not come with her. Only patients are allowed inside," the security officer informed us.

"What? There is something wrong with my wife and you expect me not to be by her side?" Just then another paralyzing wave of pain hit my body causing me to fall deeper into my husband's arms. I could barely stand up as the pain was so intense. Looking up pleadingly at my husband he withheld the rest of his argument and said, "Fine. Just help her man."

The security officer helped me into a wheelchair and wheeled me into the hospital. I've always hated hospitals. There is something about the fact that this is where so many people are experiencing their very worst days that makes me loathe coming here. Now I am the person experiencing one of my worst days and I have to do it here. Although my husband never left the hospital, he sat outside in the car, I had to do it alone. The wait to see a doctor was execrable. I sat in that room they stuffed me in for hours before the doctor finally came to examine me.

"I would like to do an ultrasound to make sure everything is ok but right now our ultrasound machines are not available. If you could come back at nine AM I will make sure you get in and everything gets checked out. For right now, I am going to send you home with a pain reliever to help you get through the night." And just like that, I was being wheeled out, still in insurmountable pain.

We arrived back home around midnight. It had been a super long and painful day and even with the pain relievers the doctor sent me home with it felt like my pain was only increasing. I could not sleep. I could not stand. I could not lie down. I was miserable. We had been planning for our baby since the moment I found out I was pregnant. His or her nursery was already underway and while I just had the basics in there until we found out the sex of the baby so I could decorate accordingly I did have a few furniture pieces set up including a rocking chair my favorite Tik Tok influencer suggested all new moms should have. I went into our nursery and tried to find a comfortable position in my chair.

As I sat there alone I said a silent prayer "Dear God, I don't know what is going on with my body but please protect me and my baby amen." Ending the prayer I felt a release of discharge in my panties. Running to the bathroom I checked to find I was bleeding. Panic took over me as I yelled for Nolan, "Something is wrong! Something's wrong! God please" I screamed.

Rushing to my side Nolan asked "Baby, what's wrong?"

"I don't know. I'm bleeding. We have to go back to the doctor."

Arriving back at the hospital, it was now around four AM. The ultrasound machine was still unavailable until nine AM so they told me I had to wait. Wait for them to make sure my baby is ok. Wait as the pain continued to engulf my body. Wait while chunks of blood continued to escape my body. Wait with the uncertainty of what was next for us. Was I dying? Was I losing my baby? "God please, help me," I whispered to myself.

Five hours later they finally got me in for an ultrasound.

"What's wrong? What do you see?" The doctor looked at the screen with an indecipherable expression. "Please tell me something!" I said in a barely audible voice.

The doctor looked at me and said, "The baby has no fluid surrounding him. I am sure that while you were bleeding your water broke as well. At this stage of your pregnancy, the chances of him surviving are extremely low. At this point, I am afraid to say you have two options. We can wait it out and see what happens or you can terminate the pregnancy but there is nothing more we can do to help him."

It was a boy I thought to myself. My son. I looked at the ultrasound screen as the doctor's words replayed in my mind, "There is nothing more we can do to help him."

"Can I have a moment?" I asked the doctor.

"Sure," he replied, leaving me in the room. Alone.

Picking up the phone I took a deep breath and Facetimed Nolan who was waiting in the car.

Tearfully I told him what the doctor told me, "What do we do?" I asked.

"You're in so much pain. The baby has no water surrounding it and the heart rate is lowering. I don't want to say it but I think we…I think we have to terminate," he said.

"He," I replied.

"Huh? He what?" he said through his tears.

"You called the baby it, but he's a boy. He was a boy. Our son."

We both sat silently staring at each other as our tears showered our phone screens and we mourned the loss of our son. I opted for the pills, not wanting to go under the knife. I laid in the hospital bed alone after taking the pill and with every cramp and bloodshed I experienced I felt my son's life slipping away from me. The doctor did let me see him. His little body was no bigger than the size of my hand. So many thoughts of what could have been ran through my mind as I looked at my son. So many dreams that would go unrealized. My son left my body too soon, taking a piece of my heart with him.

Alexa, play No More Drama by Mary J Blige

6.

Done Mom

Today

"Have you heard from momma?" I asked my sister Carmen when she answered my Facetime call.

"Well hello to you too Malia and no I have not heard from your mother. We haven't spoken since that last family meeting."

"That was four days ago! We all need to stop letting this ~~foster~~ *fester* and sit down and talk about everything that happened. No walking out this time. How are we supposed to move past everything and heal if we don't acknowledge it even happened?"

"Move past it and heal? See you can say that because it didn't happen to you. I'll never move past it. I'll probably never heal from it and I'll never forgive momma for letting it happen to me." Carmen replied, looking away from the phone screen as tears began to cascade down her beautiful ebony cheeks.

"Carmen, please don't cry," I said to her as my own tears began to form.

"I didn't mean it like that. You are one hundred percent entitled to your feelings about it. It is your lived experience. I'm just saying let's at least try to give momma an opportunity to explain her feelings too. I know she didn't feel good about that happening to you. She just didn't know how to explain that to you." Carmen did not look interested in anything I was saying. "Carmy," I said using the term of endearment I coined for my sister as a child. "Will you just go with me to momma's house? Seems like no one has heard from her since that meeting and I'm worried. You know she doesn't take bad news well. Let's just check on her, you don't even have to speak. Maybe, she's had time to take everything in and she'll be more receptive to a conversation. Please Carmy?"

"Fine Malia, I will meet you over there. But I am not going out of my way to initiate that conversation with her. I just want to make sure she's good, then I'm out. If she wants to acknowledge what happened she's going to have to be the one to start that conversation. She's the adult in this, I am her child."

"Understandable, I will meet you over there in 15 minutes!" I said, ending the call.

At twenty-nine I had always been the go-between for my sister and our mother. Sherri, our mom, was just sixteen when she had me and was eighteen when she had Carmen. My Father's mother took me in when I was a baby and since my teenage mother had no desire to leave the streets she did not contest. I was lucky, I was raised by my grandparents who had been married for over 50 years. My Father lived with us as well. He graduated from high school and then college and went on to start his career in investment banking. When he moved out of his parents' house he let me stay with them because that was the only home I'd known. I never wanted to leave my grandmother's side and she never wanted to leave mine. Even with me living with my grandparents, my father was and still is a prominent figure in my life. Carmen on the other hand, I'm not even sure momma knows who her dad is. Momma dropped out of high school, not like she attended much when she was in school anyway. She spent her days hanging out with corner boys getting high and living the fast life. Carmen's arrival did not slow Momma down one bit. Wherever Sherri went, Carmen went too. Momma and Carmy would often visit me at my grandmother's house and I always remembered Carmen never wanting to leave after a visit. One time I asked my grandmother if Carmen could stay with us but when she tried to have that conversation with my mom, let's just say it didn't go over well. Sherri accused my grandmother of trying to steal both of her children. Saying that she only allowed my grandmother to keep me because I had been with her since I was a baby but Carmen had been with our mother since she was a baby and she was keeping her. I could see Carmen's hopes and dreams for a stable life vanish with our mother's "no" that day. Her heart broke and I don't think it ever got mended.

After Mommy dropped out of high school, she and Carmen hit the streets. It was not unusual for Sherri to be at a party with Carmen. She would put

Carmen in a back room with some cartoons and enjoy her night. Drinking, smoking, drugs, sex, Carmen saw it all and when she came over to visit me she would tell me all the stories. But she never told me the one she told us at the family meeting, although to be honest, I wasn't surprised at what she revealed.

Four Days Earlier

"I am so glad everyone could make it to this family meeting," I said. " I have been feeling like we are all a bit disconnected and I just want us to work on being better people to each other. I am committed to being a better sister to you Carmy and a better daughter to you Mommy. I want you both to come over for Sunday dinners instead of feeling like I have to pick between you both. Carmy." I turned to my sister, " Our kids are getting older, I want them to play together more, I want them to grow up close like I wish we did." When she didn't seem to have a response I turned to our mother "Mommy, I want them to know you as their grandma. They are super close with my in-laws but I want them to know my side too!" I looked at my sister's blank expression and then our mother's, whose face was sorrowful with a glint of hope in her eyes. "Well you two, do you have any thoughts on how we can make things better?" My grandmother's recent passing made me realize how limited our time on earth truly was. All I wanted more than ever was to see the relationship between my mother and my sister mend so the three of us could be a real family. To my surprise and probably Carmen's too, our mother turned to her, grabbed both of her hands, took a deep breath, and began to speak.

"Carmen, I want you to know that I love you so much. You and your sister mean everything to me." She paused, glancing at me before continuing. "I know why you stopped talking to me all those years ago. I know I was not a good mother to you. Malia had her grandma and you, you were stuck with me. I know you saw things with me as your mother you should have never seen. Now that I am sober I am starting to remember things the drugs helped me push away. The things I exposed you to. Seeing me high or seeing me having sex so I could get high. I was a functioning addict that was on autopilot. You deserved so much better than me but I wouldn't, couldn't let you go. I couldn't lose both of my girls. I am so sorry I kept you and still put me before you."

Sherri had always been beautiful but I was starting to see the hard life she used to live show up on her face. Her hazel eyes were weighted down with dark circles and her once flawless skin was freckled with scars. Our mother looked depleted and weighed down. I could tell she was really trying with Carmen, the look in her eyes begging for Carmen's forgiveness. For Carmen to lift the weight the drugs and alcohol had once masked. However, one look at Carmen and I knew the relief our mother was hoping to find in her would not come. Carmen's long braids cascaded around her perfect heart-shaped face, moving several strands out of the way to reveal the same hazel eyes our mother held. Carmen began to speak.

"Thank you for acknowledging that you were a horrible mother to me. That your selfishness robbed me of a life with my sister and a real family." She said with a venom-laced tone I had never heard from her before. " I know you and Malia are hoping for some kumbaya, I forgive you, hug and we are instantly a family moment but I can't give you that. I can't give you that because your bullshit robbed me of not only a stable life but it robbed me of my innocence. Yeah, I saw it all but I also…" She paused looking down and taking in a deep breath, " You wouldn't let me live with Malia and her grandparents but you finally gave me away to Aunt Bertha and her pedophile of a boyfriend and you just left me there to be violated over and over again. Why wouldn't you let me stay with Malia? Why would you leave me there instead? Why did you let Malia have a real chance at life and take those same chances away from me? If you were going to keep me, why didn't you keep me? You took everything from me, my sister who I don't even like being around because she reminds me of the person I could have been. You took away my ability to have a healthy relationship because every time a man tries to get close to me I run believing he will inevitably hurt me after he gets what he wants. I can't do drugs to mask the pain because the few times I thought about it a memory of you passed out in your vomit wouldn't let me indulge. You've ruined the taste of alcohol for me by letting me taste it when I was ten. You took everything from me and even though a part of me is happy you are in a better place, another part of me thinks you could die tomorrow and I would be grateful to God for putting me out of my misery and ridding the world of a woman like you."

I had never heard silence so loud. The three of us sat there meditating on everything Carmen just said. I wanted so badly to be the one to have the words to bring them back together but Carmen's speech had left me incapable of forming a single thought. Carmen had been ordered by the court to stay with Aunt Bertha when Momma got locked up for a year. Once again, my grandmother had tried to get Carmen to stay with us, but Aunt Bertha was

Momma's next of kin and they said she had to go there instead. I never knew what my sister went through while at Aunt Bertha's. I hardly saw her during her stay there and when momma got out and took her back she never told me any stories from her time at Aunt Bertha's. I assumed that was because living with Aunt Bertha compared to living with Momma was boring and unexciting, too normal to produce the stories living with Momma produced. I had never been more devastated to be so wrong.

Mommy's golden brown skin was etched with sorrow as she fought back the tears that were on the verge of escaping at any moment. Carmen refused to make eye contact with Momma again after her speech. Finding a spot on the wall in front of her she refocused her attention into outer space and zoned out. Carmen didn't even budge when Mommy stood to her feet, looking at her with her mouth agape as if she was going to say something before deciding against it and instead walking past her right out the front door.

Today

Carmen and I stood at our mother's front door and rang the bell. After no response, I looked into the ring doorbell I had purchased for our mother last Christmas and said,

"Momma, it's me and Carmen open up." Still, there was no response. Looking into the Ring again I said, "Okay momma, I know where the spare key is so we are coming in." Picking up one of the plants our mother has on her front porch, I picked up a key and unlocked the door.

"Maybe we should just leave, either she's not here or she doesn't want to be bothered with us," Carmen said, slightly annoyed.

"Well, she is going to have to say that because the only way I am leaving is if she is not here," I replied, grabbing my sister's arm and pulling her into the dark house. Sherri had inherited the home from Aunt Bertha when she passed away. Stumbling on a side table that was placed much too close to the stairs, Carmen noted the house's dark ambiance.

"Why is it so dark in here?" She asked. "And cold, it's freezing." I called out.

"Momma are you here?" When I received no response I told Carmen "I'm going upstairs to check her room. If she's not in here then we can go." Heading up the stairs I began to feel goosebumps on my arms. Yes, the house was freezing but something didn't feel right. The door to our mother's room was shut and I knocked before slowly opening the door. "Mom?" I whispered, turning on the lights and finding our mother laying on the bed. She was dressed in a long satin nightgown, her naturally long jet-black hair swept behind her shoulders. She looked so peaceful I almost didn't want to wake her up. I was so entranced by Momma sleeping that I did not hear Carmen come into the room behind me.

"Mom!" Carmen yelled with a slight panic in her voice brushing past me to our mother's bedside. "Mom, what did you take?" she said, shaking our mother and picking up the bottle of pills on the nightstand. "Fentanyl! Oh Mom, please, wake up."

Still standing by the door I watched as Carmen tried to wake up our mother. It felt as if my own breath was leaving my body with every push Carmen placed on our mother's chest in an attempt to resuscitate her. Looking to the empty right side of the bed I spotted a folded piece of paper. Through blurry tears, I walked to the bed and picked it up, and opened it. The letter was dated 3/26/2022, that was last night. My body collapsed and I said,

"Stop Carmen, she's gone." Passing her the folded piece of paper.

"I knew I should have come over here to check on her sooner," I whispered more to myself than to Carmen.

Sherri

I lay in silence as he moved in and out of me praying it would be over soon. I can't even count how many times momma's boyfriend had taken me but I had learned not to yell and not to fight back. If I was still and quiet it ended sooner. I knew he was coming over today so I got some pills from one of my friends and took two before I went to sleep. I'm not sure what they were but luckily for me, they had already begun to hit when I heard him open my door. I felt nothing as I lay there waiting for him to finish, not even the tears that were creating a puddle on my pillow.

"You finally gave me away to Aunt Bertha and her pedophile boyfriend and you just left me there to be violated over and over again." Carmen's words echoed in my mind as memories of my own childhood trauma began to replay.

"I didn't know," I said to myself as I paced in my bedroom. "If I did know I would have killed him myself." I screamed angrily as tears filled my eyes. The weight of the guilt, shame, and failure I felt began to overtake me as I cried in my bedroom.

"You could die tomorrow and I would be grateful to God for putting me out of my misery and ridding the world of a woman like you." My daughter wants me dead and I can't blame her, I thought to myself. I was a horrible mother. She didn't deserve to have me as a mother, she deserved so much better. They both did. Through blurry eyes, I went downstairs to my kitchen grabbing a wine glass and a bottle of wine. Then I headed to my closet and took out a box from the top back corner of the shelf searching for a pill bottle I hid there that a friend gave me when I first got out of rehab. Heading back up to my room I thought if this is what will make them happy then at least I know I finally did one thing right!

Now

Opening the letter, Carmen began to read aloud their mother's last thoughts.

3/26/2022

> *9:00 pm*
>
> *I always felt invisible, I wonder if you will see me now. Now that it's too late. I finally had enough and did the thing I'd been thinking about doing for months now, hell, years if I'm being honest. This moment is very reminiscent of that scene in Being Mary Jane when Lisa finally finds the peace she's been looking for. I've got my glass of wine and an assortment of pills. I don't want to feel anything. I simply want to fade into bliss. I pray that God forgives me and that I truly forgive Him so He will let me in the gate when I arrive. I hope it's like that Tupac song Thugz Mansion and when I get there I get to find a peace that lasts and not like Rich Fontane's Heaven Review Center on Instagram even though I liked those skits.*
>
> *As I think of everything that has brought me to this moment I know I have made the right choice for me. I am so tired. Tired of trying. Tired of failing. Tired of not feeling good enough. Tired of feeling like no one cares. Tired of feeling alone, of being alone. Nothing about this life feels worth staying here for, not even my children. Maybe they will be better off now that I am gone. I always felt like I was not the mother they wanted or deserved. After that family meeting, I knew it was true. I thought the courts giving Carmen to Aunt Bertha while I was upstate would give her a glimpse of the stability I knew she had been craving but to hear that my Carmen was violated by one of Aunt Bertha's boyfriends just like I was violated by one of*

my mom's boyfriends when I was a little girl was too much. By keeping Carmen I exposed her to the generational curse the women in my family have been passing down for decades, probably longer.

I wish my life was different. Maybe where I grew up in a small town in a family home that was passed down for generations. Where I married my high school sweetheart and everyone loved and admired our love story. Maybe I watched too many romance movies, but it could have happened. The house, the dog, the white picket fence. Happiness? Unfortunately, that's not my story. I got the two baby daddies who didn't give a shit about me. One was decent enough and the other went ghost. Maybe if I had stayed with Malia's dad I would have finished high school and gone to college and been a better parent to both of my girls. But I guess if I would have stayed with him Carmen wouldn't be my baby and I just can't imagine life without her.

Carmen, please know how much I loved you. On my darkest nights when it was just you and me, you were my life. You were my smile. You were my hopes and dreams. You and Malia are the reasons I lasted as long as I did. I am so sorry I failed you. I am so sorry you both got me for a mother. I often wonder if you both will hate me. I mean you can't hate me any more than it feels like I hate myself? All I ever wanted from the moment I found out I was pregnant was to be a good mom but I was selfish and acted out of my pain. I didn't put you two first. I did not lead you the way you should go as the Bible said to. I remember holding Malia as a baby, telling my best friend I didn't want to mess her up, luckily her grandma stepped up but I am so devastated that I did just that to you, Carmen.

To my girls, I am sorry I let you down. Sorry, I couldn't be the mother you wanted me to be. That I hoped to be. Maybe now that I am gone you will have the freedom to live your very best life without the weight of the generational curses I bore you with, holding you down. This was not because of you. I was just too weak to go on. I pray you are stronger than me. That my weakness didn't pass down to you. You may not understand what I feel right now and I pray you never will.

To everyone else don't be making a fool of yourselves at my funeral crying and carrying on talking about you'll miss me. Where have you been all these years when I was crying out for help with no response? Do you feel bad? Will you be there for my girls?

Do you see me now?

Now that I'm gone?

Sherri

I curled up next to my mother, placing my head on her shoulder.

"I saw you momma," I whispered silently, my tears staining her nightgown. "I always saw you."

Standing by the bed, Carmen let the letter slip through her hands. She slowly backed away from me and Momma until her back hit a wall. Sliding down until she was sitting on the floor taking in me crying into our dead mother's shoulder.

Barely above a whisper, I heard, "I didn't mean it," escape from Carmen's lips.

We stayed in that room, Carmen on the floor and me on the bed, paralyzed under the weight of the finality of death, under the grief of what could have been and would never be, and silently grieved the loss of our mother.

Hey Google, play SuperFriend by Faith Evans, Keke Wyatt, Monifah, Nicci Gilbert, and Syleena Johnson

7.

Moms that Brunch

"Hey, beautiful ladies!" Hailey said as she arrived late to brunch as usual. "I would say sorry I'm late but you hoes should be used to that by now so I'm not," she said as she blew kisses to her friends before taking her seat.

Hailey, Jasmine, Sara, and Toni were meeting up for their mom's brunch. They had hoped to have this brunch once a month but life had made that more difficult than they thought with husbands, boyfriends, babies, testy teens, demanding jobs, and some of them juggling multiple jobs and varying schedules. They were lucky if they were able to meet once every six months. This was one of those rare occasions when they were all present!

"Hello, can I start you all out with any drinks?" the waiter asked, taking out his pad to take down their order.

"Bring a round of those super mimosas," said Toni.

"A round? Do you want two to share? They are 60oz, can I put a couple of straws in them?" the waiter asked.

"I love these girls but I'm not drinking off them. Four, please! Don't worry, we can all handle ourselves." Toni said and they all laughed.

Smiling, they each gave the waiter their brunch orders which consisted of Shrimp and Grits for Hailey, Salmon Benedict for Toni, Corn Beef Hash for Sara, and Chicken and Waffles for Jasmine.

"I can't believe we are finally all here! It's been forever!" Jasmine said. "I am so happy Brandon's mom is in town and took the baby for a few hours so I can get out. I have been cooped up in that house for months. I feel like a milking machine. All I do is pump and suck. Brandon and the baby are wearing me out!" Jasmine was a first-time mother who was clearly still adjusting to motherhood. Her hair was in a messy bun and her white v-neck t-shirt spotted with what looked like smashed peas peeked through her black cardigan.

"Pump and suck?" asked Sara.

"I haven't been in the mood for sex lately but my head game is still impeccable. A little suck will get him off my back, literally. My mouth puts him to sleep and my breast puts his son to sleep." The ladies all laughed.

"Girl you better give that man some, it's been 7 months since you had the baby." Toni chimed in.

"Girl, I think my vagina is broken." Jasmine replied,

"Has it had enough?" Hailey asked. Hailey, Sara, and Toni looked at each other before singing in unison, "Broken Pussy" from the first episode of season one of Insecure.

Jasmine laughed, "I really hate you guys."

"For real Jas, it's not uncommon for a woman's sex drive to drop after she's had a baby. Your hormones are still settling, your pussy ain't broken girl, and speaking of pussy, I am having the opposite problem." Sara said, taking in a huge sip of her mimosa. "I am getting worn out every day and I am loving it." Her gold hoop earring swung as she flipped her black and brown ombre tresses out of her face exposing her beautiful smile.

"Since when you got a man?" Toni asked her.

"Since I got my second job, working overnights at the warehouse. I needed some extra money so I took an extra shift and met Gerald," she explained.

"Does Gerald have a big dick? He sounds like he has a big dick." Toni inquired as they all leaned in a little closer to hear Sara discuss her new beau's dick game.

"I ain't been serviced like this in…damn, never. It's so good I invited him over one night and I forgot DJ was home. DJ is usually with his dad on the weekends but this night I forgot he skipped because he had some tournament to go to the next day that his dad couldn't take him to. I was screaming so loud DJ ran into my room thinking I was dying or something and saw his momma face down ass up. It's been weeks and that boy still ain't looking at me the same."

Sara described covering her face with her elaborately painted and bedazzled nails.

"Bish, what!? DJ saw you having sex?" Jasmine asked louder than necessary just as our waiter arrived to drop off our food. "I would be mortified," Jasmine whispered once the waiter left, clutching her imaginary pearls.

Toni and Hailey couldn't contain their laughter. "What did you do?" They asked, clearly amused by the story.

"I tried to talk to him but he went into his room, locked the door, and wouldn't let me in. And I was mortified but Gerald calmed me down…" She took a deep breath before finishing her sentence, "With his head between my legs" She said with a grimacing face that mimicked the emoji that showed all the teeth.

"I know you did not go back in that room and finish Sara!" Jasmine asked in disbelief.

With slight hesitation, Sara replied, "I swear I was so quiet, and as soon as we finished I made him go home."

"Girl, I can't," was Jasmine's response.

"Well I can," Toni said, still laughing as she reached over to Sara to slap her five. "Like these kids need to learn to not come barging in our rooms. They don't pay for nothing up in that house. Knock first or you might see something you wish you hadn't like your momma getting her back broke."

"Okay okay," Sara said "Let's change the subject. This is bringing up conflicting feelings. I don't know whether I should call Gerald or beg DJ for his forgiveness." Sara said.

"It's crazy how fast these kids are growing up. DJ knew what you were doing. Shoot he is probably doing it too." Jasmine said. "All of you with these teenagers and here I am starting from scratch. I'm scared for him to grow up. I just want to keep him as my little baby forever."

"Cherish this time, these teenage years aren't for the faint of heart." Hailey chimed in. "Daily Savannah has me ready to drop her back off at the Kaiser Permanente Medical Center I gave birth to her at. Like Hello, she's defective and I need my extended warranty or something. Help a sista out."

"You still having issues with Savannah, Hailey?" Toni asked.

"It's like the older this girl gets, the more difficult she becomes and the more I realize…" She took a deep breath and confessed "Y'all I don't like being a mom"

"Hailey, you have a teenage daughter, no mom of a teenage daughter likes being a mom during that phase." Toni said.

"No, I am for real. I really don't like it and haven't for a while. Sometimes I wonder how different my life would be if I didn't have her. I feel like she's holding me back. I used to have dreams, things I wanted to do, and places I wanted to go. I had to sacrifice it all for her. Don't get me wrong, I love her. Like she is the only person in the world I would ever consider doing a bid for. I'm straight telling on everybody else but for her, I'd do life in prison. But I still feel like nothing I do is good enough for her. Sometimes being around her feels like being around a stranger on the street. We're uncomfortable and barely have anything to say. She's ungrateful, lazy, and entitled. I give and give and this girl makes me feel like a bad mother at every turn. I just want to live my life. I want to travel, date, and work a passion job instead of this wack ass 9 to 5, I want my back blown out too, I even want to suck, but you can keep that pump mess I'm done having kids. I don't know guys, more and more I think I am starting to resent her. Like she took my dream life from me." Hailey paused, taking in her friend's speechless expressions. "I know I know, I'm a bad person. A bad mother." Hailey's impeccably made-up face held a somber gaze. She was the big personality of the group but hardly ever was one to be this vulnerable, her friends just needed a moment to take in her honestly.

Breaking the awkward silence Jasmine said, "Dang, Hailey. I know I am the new mom and I was just complaining about him sucking the life out of me but I hope I never get to the point of resenting my baby."

"Okay Jas, that's not helpful!" Toni chimed back in. "Parenting is hard. Being a single parent is hard. I don't know about the rest of the girls but I have def imagined what my life would look like without these little minions." They all nodded in agreement. "That doesn't make you a bad person or mother. That makes you human! It's not always going to be easy but you make a choice every day to show up for her, to be present even when you wish you didn't have to, and to give even when she chooses not to receive. She may not see it now, may not appreciate it now but she will be grateful for your sacrifices later." Toni hugged Hailey who had tears in her eyes. "Ugh, I did not come here for this sappy shit," Hailey said, dotting the sides of her eyes and trying to preserve her mascara as Toni held her close. "Y'all know I'm a thug and now I am over here leaking mimosa from my eyes." They all laughed. "Thanks, Toni, seriously. This has been a rough few months, hell years with her. Right now I am counting down the days until her butt is up out of my house and off to college. "Just 1,097 days to go!" Hailey said matter of factly.

"Not you having a countdown." Sara laughed.

"Trust sis, I have been there. Donnie gave me a run for my money. I couldn't wait for his butt to leave for college. That day came and I was a complete mess. I must have cried for a week straight." Toni said.

"A week? Girl, you got six other kids at the house." Sara said with a confused grin.

"And my favorite, most reliable, cheapest—because I didn't have to pay him— babysitter just left for college," Toni said laughing.

At 5'2, Toni might have been the smallest in the group of ladies but she was also the mom's mom of the group. Toni knew what to say to make you laugh, make you think, provide you with comfort, and give you the best advice. She was the group's nucleus.

"I know I have been here for all your kids Toni but I still don't know how your little butt pushed out seven boys. Your pussy is the one that should be broken." They all laughed.

"Please, girl around number three they started crip walking up out of here."

These were the moments that solidified their friendship. They could laugh, cry, and be themselves together. They may not have been able to get together as much as they liked, but every time they did get together, it was like they picked right back up from where they started.

Amid all the laughter Jasmine's purse began to vibrate. Pulling her phone out she rolled her eyes as she read her text from Brandon. "Alright ladies, looks like my time is up. Brandon's mom ran to the store and I swear this man freaks out every time he is alone with the baby. He thinks he is going to break him or something," she said, sighing exasperatedly. "I love you, ladies! Can't wait to do this again next month!" She said, packing up her things.

Toni and Sara agreed "Yeah guys, let's try to do this again next month. I'll make time," Sara said.

"I miss this."

"Same" Toni replied.

"I miss y'all too but you know it will be a good 6 months before we will all get together again. I don't know why y'all are frontin'," Hailey laughed.

Just then *Hrs & Hrs* by Muni Long began to play from Sara's phone interrupting their goodbyes and they all looked at Sara.

"Now, I know you ain't give night shift Gerald that ringtone. You are really sprung!" Hailey said.

"Welp on that note, it's been, real ladies. Love yall." Sara said heading for the door.

"I know that's right, get some for me!" Hailey yelled out.

Toni nudged her friend with a wide smile on her face, "Hailey, can you at least wait until we are out of the restaurant?" Toni asked with a chuckle.

"Shoot, they can get some for me too," Hailey said, referencing the patrons in the restaurant. Toni grabbed Hailey and they walked out arm and arm fully amused and grateful for super mimosas with friends!

Hey Siri, play Superwoman by Alicia Keys

8.

Supermom

Jenna sat down at her kitchen table with her French vanilla coffee going over her calendar in preparation for the day's events. It was 5:15 AM and that meant she had about forty five minutes before the kids woke up to get ready for school. It was Wednesday so Kylie had to be at school early for her band rehearsal in preparation for the winter concert. Later that day Tia would need to be dropped off at dance class and Brandon had track practice. The PTA moms had a lunch meeting to go over ways to increase the winter festival sales and Jenna volunteered to host and cook. Sandy was so picky about store-bought food and Violet only ate organic gluten-free vegan options while Betsy always wanted an assortment of potato chips and soda. After Jenna dropped off Kylie she would swing by the store to pick up the PTA lunch items before coming home.

Jenna had always dreamt of the life she was living now. A life with a loving husband whose job afforded her the ability to be a stay-at-home mother to their three children. She imagined their custom-built home, a Spanish-inspired colonial house, which she decorated with a mix of modern and traditional decor to give a warm and welcoming atmosphere. Every picture frame, accent rug, end table, and sofa was an intentional choice. Jenna wanted her family to be at peace when they walked through the doors of their home. She wanted the home to be a place of comfort and safety since growing up, Jenna's home was anything but that. Jenna was just 10 years old when her father left her mother and started a new family. Her mother was so busy working multiple jobs to keep the lights on, she never had time to invest in what Jenna had going on. The void she felt from her father's absence and her mother's emotional abandonment is something Jenna vowed her husband and children would never feel. She would be the best wife and the most attentive mother. She would not fail her family the way she felt her parents failed her.

Having a pretty good idea of how her day would go, Jenna took one last sip of her coffee before getting up to make the kids breakfast. Whipping up some blueberry pancakes, eggs, and sausage, and setting them neatly on the table in preparation for their arrival downstairs.

"Good Morning honey?" her husband said as he came up behind her wrapping his arms around her waist and kissing her neck.

Turning to face him Jenna said, "Good morning baby, would you like breakfast?"

Grinning he replied, "If the breakfast is you!"

Looking at the clock on the kitchen stove it was now 5:45 AM, Jenna had fifteen minutes before the kids would be up and her day would officially begin.

"We'd have to make it fast," she replied.

"Well, you could just…you know." She knew what he wanted.

Smiling, she said fine and walked with him to the downstairs bathroom. Her husband quickly dropped his pants, lowered the toilet seat cover, and sat down. Jenna dropped to her knees and took him into her mouth. Ten minutes later Jenna was cleaning herself up in the mirror while he pulled up his pants.

"Thank you, baby," he said, kissing her on the cheek and leaving the bathroom.

"I'll see you after work." He yelled. "Hey, can we have pot roast for dinner?" He said as he headed towards the door running into Kylie. "Hey baby girl?" He smiled at his daughter, kissing her on the forehead and saying "Have a great day," before disappearing out the door.

"Mom," Kylie said entering the kitchen. "Don't forget I have to be at school in fifteen minutes for band practice."

"I didn't forget Kylie. Now have a seat and eat please" Jenna knew it would take her five minutes to drive to the school and drop Kylie off. By the time she would get home Tia and Brandon would be eating breakfast and she would have thirty minutes before it would be time to take them to school. Every day Kylie acted as if her mother was oblivious to her ever-changing schedule when in actuality Jenna made it a point to know every move each member of her family made before they made it. Her calendar was her best friend and no detail of each of her children's and husband's day was not accounted for. Organization was key to being a good mom and wife!

Once all the kids were dropped at their respective schools, Jenna went to Kroger grocery store to grab the PTA lunch and a pot roast for dinner. Kroger was like a second home to Jenna, gliding through the aisles, the groceries practically floated into her cart.

Approaching self check out Jeanna paused when she heard, "Jenna, is that you?" Turning to see Kathy Gershum.

"Oh hey, Kathy!" Jenna said, putting on her best fake smile. She hadn't liked Kathy since she complained to the track coach that Brandon was getting special privileges that her son wasn't getting just because Jenna and her husband were good friends with the coach and his wife. The reality was Brandon was just the best track star on the team but Kathy insisted this conflict of interest was affecting the morale of the team threatening to tell the Superintendent if her son didn't get to be the anchor in the relay race during the rival game, a spot reserved for Brandon.

"Soooo glad I ran into you because I was totally going to call you. I was thinking that since the track season is winding down we should start planning the end-of-season party. You know we have to celebrate Kevin and the team winning the rival game!" Kevin and the team? He didn't win that meet by himself I thought.

"Yeah, we totally should celebrate the team. Let me know what you think up. I have to run!" Jenna said, trying to walk away.

"Actually, I was thinking you could take the lead. You know since you have more time on your hands being a stay-at-home mom and all. I totally would help but I am just so exhausted with work. Corporate America is a doozy, you're so lucky you don't have to worry about anything except your kids and shopping. Let me know what you think up. I gotta run, I got a meeting back at the office. So excited to see what you come up with! Bye," She said, running off before Jenna could get a word in.

Jenna stood for a moment stunned. Never mind the fact that she couldn't stand Kathy, she hated when people, women in particular, acted like being a stay-at-home mom was not a job. Kathy was at the store in the middle of the day just like Jenna was but because she had "a meeting back at the office" she felt like she could look down on Jenna. And to put the end-of-track party on Jenna as if her life was way too busy to plan it herself. Jenna let out a deep breath and reached for her phone to put "plan end of track season party" in her calendar, when she noticed the time. She hurriedly finished her shopping and headed home for the PTA meeting.

Later that evening Jenna found herself back at her kitchen table longing for a glass of wine but instead with a cup of water as she helped Tia finish up her homework.

"How are my beautiful girls?" her husband said as he entered the kitchen walking straight to the microwave. Without even looking inside he pressed the 3-minute button knowing Jenna had already placed his plate inside. "What are you two working on?" He asked.

"Vocab. I hate vocab Daddy, why do we have to learn to spell hard words anyway?" Tia answered, "Can't you and Mommy just read me the hard words?"

"Well, sweetheart daddy isn't always going to be around to read you the hard words, and what if mommy is busy making dinner or cleaning the house or something? Don't you want the independence to read it on your own?" he asked her.

"No" she replied with a straight face and he couldn't help but laugh.

"Hey, it's getting late. Why don't you run upstairs and get ready for your bath," Jenna said to Tia and the little girl happily left the table and skipped up the stairs.

"Thanks for the food babe, I've been thinking about this pot roast all day." He said. "You know what else I've been thinking about?" He tried and failed to look seductive as he put a fork full of roast in his mouth. "Maybe we can finish what we started this morning."

Jenna was exhausted from her day but she was a firm believer that you should never turn down your husband and that was a motto she lived by.Getting up from the table Jenna started walking towards the stairs without looking back she said, "As long as it starts with you on your knees first this time."

Hey Google, play One Mo
Gen by Mariah Carey

9.

Mom's Night Off

"Yeah Daddy, just like that" I moaned as he sucked my clit sending shock waves throughout my body. I needed this. I deserved this. I was going to milk this man for every ounce of pleasure he could provide me with!

"Wait," I said, getting up from the chair. "Go lay on the bed, I want to feed you."

He looked up at me with a mischievous grin "As you wish baby," He said as he walked over to the bed and lay down.

I took a long look at his 6'4 frame. His body looked like it had been dipped in midnight and then chiseled to perfection by every Roman god. I mounted his face and took a seat. I wanted to fuck his nose just like Trina talked about in the song "Look Back At It." I grinded on his face, clinching the headboard for support. Back and forth I slid while his tongue took turns grazing my clit and entering me. At one point I thought he might have been gasping for air as he dug his low-cut nails into my butt cheeks but I didn't care. I kept my stride gliding back and forth on his face as the pressure mounted inside of me until I could no longer contain it, leaving my essence all over his face.

I slid off his face working my way down to his chest and then to his penis which was standing at full attention.

"How many times do you think you can make me cum tonight?" I asked licking my climax off his lips.

He replied, "How long do we have again?"

"You have to be gone by nine AM, that's when my momma is dropping the kids off and she won't be late."

"Well it's only midnight, that means we have nine hours," he answered.

"Let's make that a cute eight, seriously if anything that lady will be early," I replied.

"Fine," he said, "eight hours to make you cum eight times, at least," he said, kissing my neck.

"You think you can give me an orgasm for an hour for the next eight hours?" I said laughing.

"One down and seven to go," he said as he flipped me to my back and climbed on top of me.

"Are you ready?" he said, kissing my breath away.

"Yes," I said, completely surrendering to whatever he had in mind.

Taking his penis in his hand he rubbed the head against my womanly folds. Still moistened from my face ride, I spread my legs wider begging him to enter me. I closed my eyes in anticipation and was surprised when I felt his wet tongue circling my anus as his fingers entered me.

"When did he get down there?" I thought to myself before the titillation of his fingers and tongue moving in sync inside of me as if they were dancing a choreographed number caused my mind to blank. His fingers pumped in and out of the honey pot while his thumb pressed against my clit and his tongue lapped circles around my bootyhole. *In out swipe lick, In out swipe lick* "Ahhhhh" I screamed out in pleasure "Please baby," was all I could whimper before succumbing to the most blissful orgasm. A man of his word, he spent the rest of the night, well morning, exploring my body. No nook or crevice went undiscovered as he gave me 3, 4, 5, 6, 7, and finally, 8 orgasms as promised. I held on to each orgasm as if I was a bear during the hyperphagia phase before hibernation. Who knows when my mother would take all the kids again? The memories of this night would surely last me through the winter.

I wasn't sure how long I had been sleeping when I was awakened by an angry knock on my door. I looked at the clock on my nightstand, "crap" I said when I saw it was 8:45 am, I knew she would be early, I thought to myself. Turning in the bed I was getting ready to tell him to hide when I realized I was in bed alone. Just then my phone rang, I didn't need to answer it to know it was my momma outside the door wanting to drop off the kids. I picked up the phone, ignoring my mom's ringtone and instead reading a text.... from him.

"Call me the next time you have a babysitter, smirking emoji." I smiled as the banging in the background continued.

"Coming momma." I yelled, climbing out of the bed and reaching for my t-shirt and panties that lay on the floor next to my bed. Each wobbly step to the door sent flashbacks of last night through my brain and straight to my still throbbing pussy. I opened the door with my best "I am so sorry I kept you waiting momma" face knowing that playing nice would get her to babysit again. Until then, the memories of one through eight would have to hold me over.

Made in United States
North Haven, CT
22 May 2024

52800226R00036